# I Got the Christmas Spirit

Connie Schofield-Morrison · ILLUSTRATED BY Frank Morrison

BLOOMSBURY
CHILDREN'S BOOKS
NEW YORK  LONDON  OXFORD  NEW DELHI  SYDNEY

To the joys of my life: Nyree, Tyreek, Nia, Nasir, and Tiffani
—C. S.-M.

To my children, Nyree, Tyreek, Nia, Nasir, and Tiffani. Be good, be great!
—F. M.

BLOOMSBURY CHILDREN'S BOOKS
Bloomsbury Publishing Inc., part of Bloomsbury Publishing Plc
1385 Broadway, New York, NY 10018

BLOOMSBURY, BLOOMSBURY CHILDREN'S BOOKS, and the Diana logo are trademarks of Bloomsbury Publishing Plc

First published in the United States of America in September 2018
by Bloomsbury Children's Books

Bloomsbury books may be purchased for business or promotional use. For information on bulk purchases please contact
Macmillan Corporate and Premium Sales Department at specialmarkets@macmillan.com

Library of Congress Cataloging-in-Publication Data
Names: Schofield-Morrison, Connie, author. | Morrison, Frank, illustrator.
Title: I got the Christmas spirit / by Connie Schofield-Morrison ; illustrated by Frank Morrison.
Description: New York : Bloomsbury, 2018.
Summary: As she and her mother enjoy the sights and sounds of the holiday season,
a young girl feels the Christmas spirit in every jingle, yum, and ho ho ho.
Identifiers: LCCN 2017052600 (print) • LCCN 2017060462 (e-book)
ISBN 978-1-68119-528-5 (hardcover) • ISBN 978-1-68119-529-2 (e-book) • ISBN 978-1-68119-530-8 (e-PDF)
Subjects: CYAC: Christmas—Fiction.
Classification: LCC PZ7.S3682 Iaad 2018 (print) | LCC PZ7.S3682 (e-book) | DDC [E]—dc23
LC record available at https://lccn.loc.gov/2017052600

Art created with oil on canvas
Typeset in Elroy and Platsch
Book design by Yelena Safronova
Printed in China by Leo Paper Products, Heshan, Guangdong
2 4 6 8 10 9 7 5 3 1

All papers used by Bloomsbury Publishing Plc are natural, recyclable products made from wood grown in well-managed forests.
The manufacturing processes conform to the environmental regulations of the country of origin.

To find out more about our authors and books visit www.bloomsbury.com and sign up for our newsletters.

I woke up to the spirit of the season.

RISE AND SHINE!

I heard the spirit in the air.

DING DONG DING

I've been saving the spirit
all year long.

JINGLE JINGLE

I sang the spirit from my heart.

I tasted the sweet
spirit crunch!

YUM YUM

I shivered as the spirit
nipped my nose.

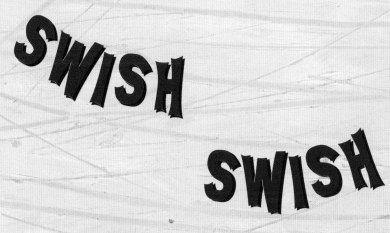

I swirled and twirled
around the spirit.

SWISH

SWISH

I sparkled in the
spirit of the lights.

I felt the spirit deep down in my soul.

I chased the spirit through the store.

I spread the spirit
with my smile.

The spirit is here!

THE SPIRIT IS YOU!

The spirit is to discover
something new.

Peace for all, good tidings, and cheer—
let's live the spirit every day of the year.